The
Bully
Bug

Starscape Books by David Lubar

NOVELS

Flip

Hidden Talents

True Talents

MONSTERRIFIC TALES

Hyde and Shriek

The Vanishing Vampire

The Unwilling Witch

The Wavering Werewolf

The Gloomy Ghost

The Bully Bug

NATHAN ABERCROMBIE, ACCIDENTAL ZOMBIE SERIES

My Rotten Life

Dead Guy Spy

Goop Soup

The Big Stink

Enter the Zombie

STORY COLLECTIONS

Attack of the Vampire
Weenies and Other Warped
and Creepy Tales

The Battle of the Red Hot
Pepper Weenies and Other
Warped and Creepy Tales

Beware the Ninja Weenies
and Other Warped and
Creepy Tales

The Curse of the Campfire
Weenies and Other Warped
and Creepy Tales

In the Land of the Lawn
Weenies and Other Warped
and Creepy Tales

Invasion of the Road
Weenies and Other Warped
and Creepy Tales

Wipeout of the Wireless Weenies
and Other Warped and Creepy Tales

The Bully Bug

A MONSTERRIFIC TALE

DAVID LUBAR

A Tom Doherty Associates Book
New York

THE BULLY BUG

Illustrations by Marcos Calo

Designed by Nicola Ferguson

A Starscape Book
Published by Tom Doherty Associates, LLC
175 Fifth Avenue
New York, NY 10010

www.tor-forge.com

The Library of Congress Cataloging-in-Publication Data
is available upon request.

ISBN 978-0-7653-3082-6 (hardcover)
ISBN 978-1-4299-9313-5 (e-book)

Starscape books may be purchased for educational, business, or promotional use. For information on bulk purchases, please contact Macmillan Corporate and Premium Sales Department at 1-800-221-7945, extension 5442, or write specialmarkets@macmillan.com.

First Edition: September 2014

0 9 8 7 6 5 4 3 2 1

For my writer and illustrator friends,
who know how hard this is,
and how easy

Contents

Author's Note

I've always been a fan of monsters. As a kid, I watched monster movies, read monster magazines, built monster models, and even tried my hand at monster makeup for Halloween. Basically, I was a creepy little kid. It's no surprise that, when I grew up and became a writer, I would tell monster stories. I've written a lot of them over the years. My short-story collections, such as *Attack of the Vampire Weenies and Other Warped and Creepy Tales,* are full of vampires, werewolves, ghosts, witches, giant insects, and other classic creatures. The book you hold in your hands is also about a monster. But it is different from my short stories in a wonderful way. Let me explain.

Years ago, I decided I wanted to tell a tale through

the eyes of a monster. That idea excited me, but it didn't feel special enough by itself. Then I had a second idea that went perfectly with the first one. What if a kid became a monster? Even better—what if the kid had to decide whether to remain a monster, or to become human again? The result of these ideas was not one book, but six. It seems the town of Lewington attracts a monsterrific amount of trouble. To find out more, read on.

The
Bully
Bug

One

A FREE SURPRISE

Bud found the box of cereal. If I'd found it, none of this would have happened. I'm smarter than Bud. He stayed back twice. I only got kept back once. But with him staying back twice, we ended up in the same grade. So we'll be in school together for a while, unless he gets held back again. Bud and Lud, that's us. Mom's good with poetry. Anyway, you can see I'm smarter, both because Bud stayed back more, and because of what he did with the box.

"Cereal!" Bud shouted. He'd pushed over one of Dad's washing machines. Dad collects machines. It's like a hobby and a job rolled all into one. *A machine's something you can trust.* That's what Dad says. He loves anything with a motor. Whatever machine someone throws out, Dad'll pick it up. No matter how broken it is, Dad can fix it. He keeps most of them in the backyard. We've got a couple acres fenced in behind the house. There are washers and dryers, lots of refrigerators—with the doors taken off the older ones, so nobody gets stuck inside. There's ovens, too. My sister, May, used to love playing house in the backyard. She could pretend to cook, and do all sorts of stuff.

There's cars, of course. Cars are the best machines in the world. Cars and planes are the best. We don't have any planes. Maybe someday. Though I've never seen anyone throw out a plane. Wouldn't that be cool—to see a plane sitting out on the curb next to the trash cans?

Anyway, we'd just watched this movie about a giant ape that destroys New York. It was a real old movie, but pretty good, even though you could tell the ape was fake. The ape knocked over anything that got in his way. So Bud was stomping around, thumping his chest, and knocking stuff over. Bud kind of gets wrapped up in whatever movie he's seen. I guess he was pretending the stuff was buses and buildings. Bud tipped over a washing machine and found this old box under it. The box was half rotted on the outside. You could barely read the label. Not that I do much reading, but labels aren't so hard.

"All right!" Bud shouted, suddenly stopping his ape act. "Snack time."

"Leave it alone, Bud," I said. "It's old. It's probably spoiled. And it's got that junk on it from the barrels." I pointed to the oily green puddle. This guy who'd come through town driving a big old truck gave Dad a bunch of these metal barrels for free. The problem was, someone had left all this gooey stuff in the barrels, and they leaked a lot. It must have been nasty stuff, because it killed all the grass it touched.

"Cereal can't spoil, you idiot," Bud said. "They make it so it'll last forever."

"You're the idiot," I told him. "And that's a fact."

"You are," he said back.

I let it go. I'm not much for arguing with words, and I couldn't think of a good answer. But I warned him again. "Let it be, Bud," I told him. "Just leave it alone."

"Might have a prize," he said, picking up the box by the one corner that wasn't soaked in slime. "Lots of cereal comes with a prize. Could be a race car or something. . . ."

Now, that was different. I hadn't thought how there could be something besides cereal in the box. Which doesn't mean Bud's smarter. Just means I'm less greedy. I can walk by something even if there's a prize in it. Bud, he's got to stick his finger in every coin slot in the

15

world. Can't pass by a gumball machine without checking for money someone forgot. And he sends in all the sweepstakes stuff Mom and Dad get in the mail. I told him that just means we'll get more mail. He doesn't care. But we sure do get more mail. Tons of it. Doesn't matter. Dad burns just about everything we get in the woodstove. Except for his car magazines. *Ain't nothing good ever came to me with a stamp on it.* That's what Dad always said. He knows lots.

Anyway, Bud picked up the box, and right away I could tell there was something wrong. The front was all puffed up, kind of bulging out like Uncle Ernie's stomach after we finish Thanksgiving dinner. Or any other time, for that matter, when it comes to Uncle Ernie's stomach bulging. "Careful with that," I told Bud. "It ain't right." I could swear the box looked like it was moving, but I knew that couldn't be true.

"You just want me to leave it so you can sneak back later and steal the prize," Bud said. "You want it all to yourself."

"Do not," I said.

"Do, too," he said.

I let it go. It was starting to sound like an argument. Clem and Clyde—they're older—they argue a whole bunch. Neither one of them has enough sense to back down. It drives me crazy. So I try not to argue.

Bud grabbed the top of the box and started to rip it

loose. I could have told him that was a truly stupid thing to do. The glue on top held for a second, but then the whole thing came apart so fast, it sort of exploded. The box ripped from corner to corner, and the cereal went flying all over me.

Except it wasn't cereal making the box puff up. It wasn't cereal that went flying all over me. It was a whole lot worse than that.

Two

WHAT'S EATING YOU?

It happened awful fast. I mean, it was so fast, and so awful, that at first I didn't even believe what hit me. Bugs! A box full of bugs. They smacked me all over—in the chest and on the face. I started to shout. I wasn't scared. Just surprised. Nothing scares me. But I sure was surprised to get covered with bugs. I shut up fast when one tried to crawl from my cheek into my open mouth.

I started swatting them off. Bud, idiot that he could be, just stood there for a moment. His mouth was open. It was wide open. Heck. That's just about always the case. He eats with it open. Makes me sick sometimes. Sleeps with it open. Breathes with it open. Of course, right now it was safe for him to have his mouth open.

He wasn't covered with bugs. I thought about throwing one into his mouth, but I was kind of busy getting them off me.

Finally, it sank in for Bud that I could use a hand. Better yet, two hands. He helped me swat at them. Even that wasn't the greatest help. More than once he swatted them onto me instead of off. They snapped at first, when you hit them, like pretzel sticks. The thin ones, not the real thick ones. Then they squished. Once they got squished, they stopped crawling, but I still had to pick them off my shirt. It was like peeling off dried blobs of glue.

They were biting me, too. All over my chest. Not bad, like wasps can sting, but kind of like mosquitoes. It didn't feel good, but I've felt worse. I went with Dad once to visit this friend of his who owned a real nice scrap yard. That man had a dog who grabbed on to my leg right above the ankle. Now, that's a bite. Took Dad and his friend a couple minutes to pry those jaws apart. Next to that, this was nothing. Except it was a lot of nothings. Hundreds. We must have brushed and swatted for five or ten minutes before we got rid of all the bugs.

"Wow. That was awful," Bud said, like he was the one who'd suffered.

I stared down at the torn-up cereal box. All the bugs had crawled out of it. They skittered under another washing machine. Now that I had time to look at them, I saw they were like some kind of big beetle. Sort of like a cockroach, too, but rounder. Except the head was more like a fly head. Maybe it was a fly-beetle. Guess you could call it a fleetle. Hey, that was funny. Just as funny as a joke one of the smart kids would make. I make good jokes a lot. But I don't tell them to anyone, because I hate it if people laugh at me. I mean, if I tell a joke, how can I know what they're laughing at? It might be the joke they think is funny. But they might be laughing at me because they think I'm stupid. Then I'd have to hit them. Which would get me in trouble. So I keep my jokes to myself, except I share them with Bud.

I looked at Bud so I could tell him the joke. Whoa! For an instant, I saw a billion Buds. It was like the world was made of Bud Mellon wallpaper. Now, there's a scary thought. But then I blinked real hard and everything was fine. I checked my shirt again, to make sure there weren't any more bugs on me. As far as I could tell, they were all gone.

"What do you want to do now?" Bud asked. He stared down at the box, too.

I knew what he was thinking. And I sort of felt bad for him. "Sorry you didn't find a prize," I told him. Bud expects the world to give him stuff. It doesn't work that way. Nobody gives you much, if anything. But Bud is a hopeful person.

"Thanks," he said. "Want to go climb the ovens?"

"Sure." We had a mountain of ovens out near the back fence. Dad was always warning us to stay off them, but they were pretty solid. A friend of his brought in a crane he'd borrowed from work and helped stack them up real nicely, just like a pyramid. We climbed them a lot. It was like having a jungle gym in the backyard. But this was better, because there were tons of knobs to turn, and doors to open. We used to play hide-and-seek there all the time when we were little. Since I got my last growth spurt, I can't hide in an oven anymore.

"Sorry about the cereal," Bud said when we reached the top. "I didn't mean to get you all covered with bugs."

"That's okay." I stopped to pull at the neck of my T-shirt and look down at the bites on my chest. It wasn't bad. Didn't look any worse than the time I'd accidentally knocked down a beehive in the old shed behind the house.

"You mad?" he asked.

"Nope." I sat back and enjoyed the view at the top of the mountain of ovens. I could see Dad on a ladder at the side of the house, doing something with a saw. I think he was trying to put in some air vents, because the attic gets so hot. Hey, speaking about hot things, I thought of another joke. It's a good one. They call the top of the stove a range. And that's what they call a bunch of mountains, too. We were on the range

22

range. That was funny. I told Bud. He didn't get it at first. But I explained it to him and then he laughed.

I feel good when Bud laughs at a joke, though sometimes I think he doesn't get it and just laughs 'cause he knows he's supposed to. But it still feels good. As long as it's Bud laughing. As I said, I don't feel good if other people laugh at me. Of course, that doesn't happen much. At least, not if I can hear them. People in this town know better than to laugh at any Mellon. We stick together. That's what family is all about. Mess with one Mellon, you mess with us all. Of course, they talk about us, too. I hear stuff all the time. People whisper, but I've got pretty good hearing. That's how come I know so many different words for *stupid*.

But I hadn't climbed the mountain to think about other people. I'd climbed up to relax. I stretched out across two oven tops and enjoyed the sunlight. I didn't have a care or a problem in the world. Life was just fine. Just perfect.

Of course, things can change. That's a fact.

Three

FED UP

The hot sun felt so good, I guess I fell asleep and napped for a while. That's when I was hit by the most awful sound in the world.

"Dinnnnnnnnnnerrrrrrrrrrrrrr!"

It was my sister, May. She's real pretty, and she dresses great—very colorful—but she's got a voice that could peel paint off the side of a car. And she's always yelling.

"Dinnnnnerrrrrrrr!" she screeched again.

"We heard you, May!" I shouted back as I stood up.

"Race you down," Bud said. I tried to stand up, but he gave me a push, so I toppled back on my butt. Then he started climbing down real fast, like one of those monkeys you see in the zoo.

Shoot. I wasn't going to let him beat me, even if he

started out cheating. I jumped to my feet. At least, that's what I'd planned to do. Guess I jumped too hard. And not really up. More like out. Next thing I know, I realize I've leaped off the mountain of ovens and I'm shooting toward the ground.

I looked back over my shoulder as I whooshed past Bud. I stared at him. He stared at me, like he couldn't believe what he was seeing. Then I stared at the ground, which was zooming toward me real fast. I think they said in school that when something falls, it keeps going faster and faster. Back then, I couldn't understand it. Didn't make any sense. But right now, that sure seemed pretty much true.

Stupid, I said to myself.

This was going to hurt. The top of the mountain must have been a good twenty feet off the ground. Or a bad twenty feet. Up to now, the only bones I'd ever broken belonged to other people. I wondered what it would be like to have to go around with both ankles snapped. I wondered if maybe they'd just get sprained or something. And I wondered if I'd have to sit in a wheelchair or if I could use crutches. I guess you could say I was having a wonderful trip.

Turned out I wasted a lot of wondering. My feet hit the ground with a pretty solid smack. Then my knees bent just a bit. And that was it. Nothing snapped or broke. Not even a sprain.

"Cheater," Bud said when he scrambled down next to me.

"No way. I won fair and square."

"Cheater," he said again. "You're supposed to climb down."

"And you're not supposed to push," I told him.

"Dinner!" May screeched from the back door of the house. I think she likes to hear herself. No one else does. That's a fact.

I followed Bud inside. I figured I'd let him go first since he must be feeling like a real loser right now, what with not getting a prize in the cereal and then losing the race down the mountain, even after he pushed me. Besides, it's not like there was any rush. Mom always made plenty of food.

She was setting out the roast when I got to the table. "Look, Lud. I made your favorite," she said. She took the end slice—the best part, as far as I was concerned—and plopped it on my plate. Then she pointed to the fried chicken. "Made your favorite, too, Bud."

Pit—he's my little brother—also liked roast beef. He's always trying to be like me. I guess I'm a model for him or something. "Prepare to attack," he said, waving his Captain Spazmodic action figures over his plate like a superhero about to dive at a monster. Pit never goes anywhere without a couple of plastic buddies. He switched his voice, trying to make it real deep, and said, "Meet your doom."

I laughed, because I realized it could also be *Meat, you're doomed*. But I didn't say anything, since it would be too hard to explain the joke, and it was pretty noisy at the table.

Beside the roast, there was a stack of cheeseburgers—Clem and Clyde's favorite. And stew—Dad's favorite. Spaghetti for May. Rolls, of course. And potatoes. A couple vegetables.

Mom liked to cook.

I sat down and watched Clem and Clyde fight over who would get the best burger—which didn't make much sense, since they all looked about the same to me. Clem reached the stack first, but Clyde grabbed his wrist and squeezed hard enough to make him drop the burger. Then Clem threw a headlock on Clyde and they went rolling off their chairs and onto the floor. As long as I can remember, they've had this battle over seeing who can be first. It gets tiring sometimes.

"Ludlow Axelrod Mellon," Mom said, calling me by my full name, which she only did when there was trouble, "where are your manners?"

"What, Mom?" I asked. It wasn't me fighting at the table or wrestling across the floor.

"Use your fork, boy," Dad said. "Always use the right tool for the job."

I looked down at my hands. I'd been so busy watching Clem and Clyde fight that I guess I really hadn't paid any attention to how I was eating. I'd grabbed a piece of meat with my hands. I guess I'd been biting at it. Yeah—there was a big chunk out of it, and I had the taste of meat in my mouth. Funny—I hadn't even realized I was eating. We hadn't even said grace yet.

"Cool," Pit said. He dropped his action figure, grabbed a slab of beef with two hands, like he was playing a harmonica, and started chomping at it.

"Pitney," Mom warned, hitting Pit with a full first name. That's not as bad as getting a whole name—first, middle, and last—but it's not good, either.

"Lud was doing it," Pit said.

"If he jumped off a bridge, would you jump off, too?" Mom asked.

"Yup," Pit said, nodding. "We Mellons stick together."

Mom sighed and didn't say anything more about manners.

After a while, Clem and Clyde came back to the table and joined us. I guess they'd gotten all tired out from fighting. They both grabbed the top burger again and it broke in half, which is the only way they ever settle anything. Funny how a squished-up half of a burger made each of them happier than a nice unsquished whole one.

Things quieted down for a little bit. We were too busy eating to talk or argue much. Then Dad hollered, leaped from the table, and dashed across the kitchen. He stomped his foot down hard enough to shake the walls and make Mom's *Wizard of Oz* collector plates rattle where they were hanging, on the wall above the window. "Gotcha!" he shouted.

Dad hates bugs. He can spot an ant a mile away. He keeps a flyswatter in every single room in the house. He turned toward me. "Lud, get the spray."

Why did it always have to be me? "How about Bud?" I asked.

"I'm eating," Bud said through a mouthful of chicken and potatoes. I wasn't going to argue. Not while Bud had his face stuffed. I didn't want to get into a shouting match with him when his mouth was full—which it always was during dinner. I got up, climbed the steps to the second floor, then pulled down the ladder that led to the attic. Dad kept the spray in the attic because it was real dangerous stuff.

I hated it up there. It was dark and hot. And you had to be careful with the door. It was a trapdoor. And that was too true, because the handle on the inside had broken off. So if you let it close, you got trapped. Then you had to bang and wait for someone to come along and let you out. But at least the spray can was right next to the opening, so I could grab it without going inside.

I could see where Dad had cut the first vent hole, at the edge of the floor where it meets the roof. But until he put in a fan, it would stay real hot, since the air didn't move much.

Dad would probably let Bud help him put in the fan. Bud's good with tools. Heck. Everyone in the family is good at something useful. Except me. Clem and Clyde are good at sports—especially wrestling. I guess because they get so much practice on each other. Mom can cook. Dad and Bud can fix things. May can sew. Pit draws like a real artist, even though he's just five. Well, no use thinking about all the things I'm not good at. That would take way too long.

I brought the can to Dad. It was a big plastic tank with a pump on top and a long hose that had a nozzle on the end. Dad buys bug spray by the gallon. He pumped the handle a couple times, then sprayed along the floor near the window. "Getting low," he said as he shook the can.

I finished eating, then helped clean up. Tomorrow was Thursday. I still had some homework to do. Actually, I had all my homework. It tends to pile up that way. I would have stayed in the kitchen for a while, but the smell of the spray was making me dizzy. It usually doesn't do that. Until now, I'd kind of liked it.

Anyway, I went upstairs and got out my backpack. But I had a hard time that night. I mean, I always have a hard time, because a lot of the stuff they want us to do doesn't make any sense. But tonight was hard in a different way. I was supposed to read all these pages in my history book, but my eyes kept getting funny, like I was looking through one of Mom's fancy glasses—the bumpy ones we use on holidays.

"Forget it," I said, tossing the book down on my bed. "I can't do this."

I looked across the room. Bud had already gone to sleep. We have to share a room. That's pretty much okay, except Bud makes a ton of noise when he sleeps. He says I do, too. But I don't believe him. Sometimes it sounds like he's drowning in a bucket of maple syrup. Other times, it sounds like he's trying to chew a mouthful of gravel. There's no way I'd make that much noise. Hey—that's an idea for a joke. When Bud's asleep, he makes so much noise, you could say he's sound asleep. *Sound* asleep. That's a good one.

I slipped into bed. It wasn't cold, but I pulled up the sheet and wrapped it tight around my body. It felt good, being all wrapped up.

I fell asleep just fine. Usually, I don't wake up until May starts shouting. But it was still dark when I opened my eyes. "What's going on?" I said out loud when I realized that I wasn't in bed. No mattress under my body. No pillow under my head. No sheets. It didn't make any sense.

Something was very wrong.

Four

HANG ON

"What's going on?" I asked, talking quietly so I wouldn't wake up Bud. I couldn't even figure it out for a minute. There wasn't a lot of light, just a quarter moon shining through the window. I had my hands pressed against something smooth and cool. It wasn't the floor, because all the floors in the house were made of wood boards, and whatever I had my hands on didn't feel like wood. But that wasn't the strangest part.

Something was pulling at me.

Something was trying to lift me up from the floor. No, that wasn't right, either. I wasn't being pulled up. I was being pulled down.

Down?

I let my head flop back. I looked at my bed. It was

under me. No way. That meant I was holding on to the ceiling.

I jerked hard and felt my hands and feet pull off the ceiling like it was covered with glue.

I dropped straight down and hit the bed. I didn't make much noise when I smacked the mattress. But I made a huge crash when the mattress broke through the bed frame and hit the floor.

The whole house shook.

"Hey!" Bud shouted from his bed. "Quit making all that noise."

"Sorry." I was too flustered—that's one of Mom's favorite words—to argue with him. I pressed my hand against the wall, wondering whether it would stick.

Nope.

Just to make sure, I smacked my palm flat against the wall. It still didn't stick. I smacked it harder.

"Will you stop that banging!" Bud shouted.

"Sorry." I got back under the sheet and tried to figure out what had just happened. It had to be a dream. Yeah. That made sense. I'll bet the bed broke, and I just dreamed the rest. It's like that old joke about the kid who dreams he ate the world's biggest marshmallow. Then he wakes up and his pillow is missing.

Must have been a dream.

I went back to sleep.

"Time for school! Get up, Lud!"

34

I hate it when May wakes me. I jumped out of bed. That turned out to be a mistake, since my mattress was flat on the floor. I tripped over the bed frame.

Talk about waking up on the wrong side of the bed. But things got better right away. Mom made waffles for breakfast. We all like waffles, especially Mom's. She doesn't even use a mix. She makes them from scratch. *Breakfast is the most important meal of the morning.* That's what Dad always says.

After we ate, I headed off to school with Bud, Clem, Clyde, and Pit. We had to walk, since we'd gotten thrown off the bus too many times and the school sent a letter saying we couldn't ride anymore. That hardly seemed fair.

Clem and Clyde split off after a while, since they go to the middle school. Bud and Pit and I went on through town to Washington Irving Elementary. We walked Pit to the side door for his kindergarten class, then went around to the front.

"I hate this place," Bud said when we walked up the steps into school.

"Yeah." I didn't like it, either. Everyone always stared at us, because they thought we weren't as smart as them. And because we're big. I'm taller than some of my teachers. And I guess they also stared because our dad doesn't make a lot of money and because his car is old and all beat up, with one door that's a different color. But there's better things in life than being smart. And there's better things than having money or a fancy car. That's a fact.

"See you at lunch," Bud said.

"See ya." We had to split up. They'd put us in different classes. Bud had English first. I had math. I think they split us up on purpose because they don't like us. None of my teachers do. Except maybe for Ms. Clevis. She's nice. But mostly, teachers don't like me. Especially Ms. Edderly. I had her for English, and she was flunking me. That wasn't fair. I'd been speaking English all my life. It was like someone saying I'd flunked breathing or eating. It didn't make sense. But that didn't seem to make a difference to her. As I said, almost all my teachers didn't like me.

Not that anyone else in the school does, either. I'm not complaining. I've got my brothers. That's all I need. I had a girlfriend for a little while, but it didn't work out. Dawn wanted to go for bike rides and picnics. No thanks.

Well, as Dad always says, *It don't do no good crying about the past when there'll be plenty to cry about in the future*. Especially since I was about to go to my first class of the day and I didn't have my homework done.

I shoved my books into my locker and slammed the door. As I walked away, I bumped into something.

"Ooooff."

Oh no. It was that brainy little squirt. Nerdy Norman. I'd just knocked him flat. It wasn't my fault he was standing there. He looked up at me with those terrified little eyes of his, like I'd done it on purpose. He reminded me so much of a beaver with glasses, I couldn't help laughing.

I guess I should have told him I was sorry for knocking him down, but then he might start talking to me. Besides, he wasn't hurt, so there really wasn't anything to be sorry about. But I figured I'd better say something. "Watch where you're walking next time," I told him. I hadn't meant to sound so mean, but that's what came out.

He nodded. I turned away before he had a chance to say something I didn't understand. I hate those brainy kids. They're always showing off, using words like *thermodynamics* and *metaphors*, whatever that means. And they make fun of me more than anyone else. They love to say stuff I don't get. I could show him a thing or two. I could say some real clever stuff. But what's the use? I turned away from him and went down the hall.

"Another stupid day," I muttered as I walked to my desk at the back of the classroom.

I'd just gotten comfortable—at least as comfortable as I could get in one of those small chairs—when they started the morning announcements. It was the same stupid stuff they always have, about teams winning games, and kids getting special awards. I didn't pay any attention. Until the end.

Five

PLANE PROBLEMS
WITH NUMBERS

"We won't be having a play this spring," Principal Wardener said over the loudspeaker. "Instead, we're going to try something different. We're going to have a talent show. I'd like to encourage everyone to try out."

I closed my eyes for a minute when I heard that. I could see myself onstage, doing my jokes. Making everyone laugh. Telling my best jokes, just like the comedians on TV. But as soon as I had that picture in my mind, all the faces in the crowd turned mean. They laughed at me.

I slammed my fist against the desk.

"Lud, what are you doing?" Mr. Phermat, my math teacher, asked.

"Nothing," I said.

"Well, stop pounding the furniture," he told me, smiling like that was some kind of great joke. He wasn't funny. He should have said something like *Snap out of it*, since if I hit the desk hard enough, I'd snap it. Now, that would be funny. At least, I thought it would be. Or he could have said something about how I'd gained a few pounds, since I was pounding the desk. Or he could have told me to take a break.

He went up front and started the lesson, but I couldn't keep my mind on math. I kept thinking about the talent show. If I got up onstage and showed them how funny I was, people would treat me better. They'd be nice to me. But I couldn't. There was no way I could get onstage in front of everyone. No way.

"Well, Lud, can you answer the problem?"

Oh no. I looked up at Mr. Phermat. He'd been talking to me. And there was a problem written on the chalkboard. It was one of those stupid distance things, where a couple planes are flying in different directions at different times. I hated those. I just didn't get how to do them. Heck. Almost nobody could figure them out, anyhow. Except for the real smart kids.

Mr. Phermat stared at me for a moment. I knew that he knew I didn't have a clue. So it was pretty mean of him to even ask me. I opened my mouth to say, *I don't know*. If I had a nickel for every time I'd said those three words, I'd be rich.

But this time, I didn't say it. There was something about the problem. . . . I stared at the board. I'd always figured stuff like that was about numbers and math. But I realized that it was really about flying. Everything got real clear. If the first plane took off at eight, like they said, and the second one was flying twice as fast and took off two hours later, then . . .

"They cross at two fifty-eight," I said.

Mr. Phermat started to turn away from me. Then he spun back and dropped the chalk. For a minute, he stared at me. When he was done staring, he glared around at the rest of the kids. "All right, who whispered the answer to him? Did you, Norman?"

"What?" Norman the Nerd shouted, like he'd been accused of murdering the class guinea pig. "I'd never do that. Honest. You know I'm psychologically incapable of such egregious and subversive behavior under any circumstances, especially in a pedagogical environment—"

"Okay." Mr. Phermat turned away from Norman and started writing another problem on the board. Go figure. All year, he's been angry because I didn't understand anything he was teaching. When I finally gave an answer, he got even angrier. As Dad always said, *The only way you can please some people is to make them unhappy.* You got that right.

On top of all that, I didn't have a clue where the answer came from. I looked around the room. Maybe someone had whispered it to me. No. Most of the seats near me were empty, except for the one Toby Meyers sat in over to my left. He pretty much slept through class, so he didn't care who he was next to.

"All right, smart boy, try this one," Mr. Phermat said. He pointed to another problem on the board.

Airplanes again. Flying all over the place. "Two hundred miles an hour," I said, not giving it much thought.

Mr. Phermat glared around the room again. He wrote another problem on the board. This time it was just division. But a long one. With decimals, too.

"Do it," he said, tossing me the chalk.

"I can't . . . ," I said.

"Do it!"

I walked up to the board and stood there, looking at the numbers, trying to remember how to figure out division.

Behind me, they were all starting to laugh. When I heard the giggles, my brain shut down completely. I wanted to put my fist right through the board.

"What's the answer?" Mr. Phermat shouted.

"I don't know!" I shouted back.

"That's enough," Mr. Phermat said. "Take your seat. Whatever kind of trick you were pulling, I think we just put a stop to it with some simple math."

Yeah—it was enough. I tossed the chalk away and

walked to my seat. *Go ahead*, I thought as I stomped past the nerd. *Laugh, you stupid smart kid.* I really wished he'd laugh. Then I'd give him something to cry about.

He turned away from me and start flipping through his math book, like he had something important to look up. I could tell he was scared. Good.

I glared at the board. I had no idea how I'd answered those stupid problems. It had to be a lucky guess. Not that it mattered. I wasn't good with numbers. That's a fact.

At least the bell rang soon after that. I gave Toby a push and said, "Wake up."

Then I headed for my next class.

"Hey, Lud," Bud called, running down the hall toward me.

I waited for him.

"Guess what?" he asked when he reached me.

"What?"

He grinned. "This is great. Wait till you hear what I did. It's probably the biggest favor anyone's ever done for you. But that's what brothers are for."

"What?" I asked again. I knew it would take a while to find out.

He told me how great the surprise was a couple more times, then how wonderful he was, and then just when I was about ready to scream, said, "I signed you up."

"For what?"

"The talent show," he said, grinning an even bigger grin so his mouth looked like a piano. "You're all signed up. Better start practicing."

Six

A BAD SIGN

"Are you crazy?" I asked Bud. "No way I'd do that stupid show."

"You have to," Bud said.

"Why?" I couldn't see any reason to get up on a stage in front of a whole bunch of people who didn't like me and try to make them laugh.

"Ms. Edderly told us she was going to give extra credit to anyone who did an act in the show."

Oh man. If I could get extra credit from her, I could pass English. Then I wouldn't have to go to summer school. I could sleep late and go fishing and do all the things a kid is supposed to do during the summer.

"Come on," Bud said. "You'd be great. You'd be the best act in the talent show. I wasn't sure how to spell *comedian*, so when I signed you up, I just wrote that you tell jokes."

"Talent show?" I heard a mocking voice say from behind me. "You're going to be in the talent show?"

I spun around toward the voice. I knew who it was before I even looked. That show-off wise guy, Sebastian. He thinks he's so cool, just because he's got friends and stuff. Now he was grinning at me.

"You think that's funny?" I asked, taking a step toward him. I felt my right hand curl into a fist. "Do you?"

"No." He shook his head, and I could see a bit of fear in his eyes. That was more like it.

"Good." I moved a step closer to him. "Because I just might be in that stupid show."

"Sure. Hey—you'd be great. What kind of act would it be? Weight lifting?"

Oh man, I really wanted to smash him in the face. He thought he was so funny. But the last time I hit someone, I'd gotten kicked out of school for a whole week. That wasn't so bad, except Dad had been pretty angry and didn't let me watch any television at all that whole time. Besides, I can't get kicked out of school. Bud needs me around to help keep him out of trouble.

So I just said, "Yeah. I'll be in the show," and turned away from him.

Behind my back, I could hear him calling to someone, "Hey, you'll never believe this."

Now the whole place would know about it. And I'd have to do the show. If I backed out, I'd look like a fool. But if I did the show, I'd probably end up an even bigger fool.

"This is going to be great," Bud said.

Well, there was one thing I could do without getting into trouble. *Thwack!* I smacked Bud on the back of the head.

"Hey!" he shouted, but he didn't make too much of a fuss, since I knew he didn't want either of us to get into trouble. "What was that for?"

"For signing me up," I told him.

"Last time I do you a favor," he said.

"Thanks," I said.

"You're welcome," he said.

I let it go and went on to my next class. I didn't come up with any surprise answers in that one. Which was fine with me. I'd never want to be some kind of show-off anyhow. Some people think they're so smart just because they know the answers.

Then I had science. Kids were giving their reports. I hadn't done mine yet. That nerd was up front. I just couldn't seem to get away from him today. He was doing this big report on insects. Dad would have gone crazy. He'd have stomped on the jars the nerd had brought—they were filled with all kinds of bugs—and then whipped out the spray. I didn't pay too much attention. I really didn't care about bugs.

He was telling all these gross things about how bugs eat each other. And how bugs can change their shape. And how some insects stick their eggs inside other insects. It was really disgusting. He kept using these big words that nobody could possibly understand. What's the point of talking if nobody knows what you mean?

The only part I liked was watching Sebastian. I think he was scared of bugs. Every time the nerd waved around one of his jars, Sebastian looked like he was going to fly out of his seat. Hey—fly away from bugs. That's funny.

After that, it was time for lunch. I couldn't wait. I ran out of science and headed for the cafeteria. Mom packs great lunches. I like bologna and cheese on a roll with mustard. Mom makes the rolls from scratch, just like the waffles. Bud eats peanut butter every day. He has no imagination.

I was all set for a nice, quiet meal. But a minute or two after Bud and I sat down, he started gagging and pointing at me. He looked like he was going to throw up.

Seven

COMMON SCENTS

"What's wrong?" I asked.

"Yuck. You're drooling all over the place," he said. "That's really gross."

I looked down. Oh man. Bud was right. I'd drooled all over the table in front of me. Totally disgusting. And over my food. I wiped my chin. It was soaked.

"Sorry," I said to Bud.

"That's okay." He went back to eating his sandwich.

And I went back to eating mine. It was a little soggy, but that was okay.

Nothing else strange happened in the rest of my classes. Finally, school was over for the day. I was walking home with Bud when the greatest thing hit me.

"Wow, smell that?" I asked Bud.

"Smell what?" he asked.

I sniffed and looked around the street. The smell was fabulous. It seemed like fresh baked cinnamon rolls, chocolate, cotton candy, orange soda, cherry pie, and a thousand other great things, all together. I kept sniffing as I walked. The smell was so nice, it pulled me along.

"Where you going?" Bud asked.

I didn't bother to answer. I had to find the smell. It grew stronger as I moved down the street. It was so wonderful, I closed my eyes. I didn't want anything to distract me. It had to be near. The smell was so thick, it almost felt like I could slice it with a knife.

"Lud, hold on," Bud called from behind me.

I barely heard him. I stood for a moment, letting the aroma wash over me. Then I took another step. It grew stronger. Another step. I was surrounded by the glorious smell.

Wow. I bent over and sucked in a deep breath. This was fabulous.

"*Hey!*"

Someone was shouting at me.

"Get out of there, kid. Are you crazy?"

I opened my eyes. And saw where I was. I'd stepped off the curb and was leaning over with my head stuck in the back of a truck. A garbage truck.

I stared down at a mushed-up pile of crushed stuff.

Rotting food. Paper towels. Tin cans. It looked disgusting.

But it smelled like a dream.

The guy kept shouting at me.

I backed away from the truck. I hated to leave it. I hated to move away from that wonderful smell.

Thwack!

Bud hit me on the back of the head.

"Come on. Let's get out of here. That thing stinks." He grabbed my arm and started dragging me. At the same time, the guy got in the truck and drove it down the street. I stood where I was and enjoyed the aroma that was left in the air until it faded.

"What's wrong with you?" Bud asked.

I shook my head. "I don't know." And that was the truth. I didn't know. But something was wrong. That's a fact. Something was wrong with me big-time. And I had no idea what it was. "Come on," I said. "Let's go home."

"Nah, let's do something," Bud said.

"Like what?"

He shrugged. "We could go to the mall."

I shook my head. "I'm not in the mood for that."

"What about the playground?"

"No. We'll just get in a fight if we go there."

Bud nodded. "Yeah. How about we go into town?"

"Sure." I figured that would be okay.

"We can go to the old clothes place," Bud said.

"What for?" I asked.

"Find you something to wear at the talent show. You know, a fancy suit or something. Maybe a plaid jacket. Something flashy."

Thwack!

I smacked him on the back of the head. "I'm not wearing any suit," I said. "Besides, I don't even know if I'm going to do the show."

"You have to do it," Bud said.

"Why?"

"Because I signed you up. I gave my word. You know what Dad says, right?"

I nodded. "When a Mellon gives you his word, you've got his word on it." I'd heard Dad say that often enough. "I didn't give my word," I said.

"But I did," Bud said. "So you have to."

This was getting worse and worse. If he gave his word and I backed out, then I'd be making him a liar. But if I did the show, I'd make a fool of myself. I couldn't win, no matter what.

There had to be some other way out. I tried to think of a plan, but my mind didn't work that way.

As we walked into town, I thought about the things that had happened to me since yesterday. Thinking about serious stuff isn't my best thing. But it was pretty obvious, even to me, that my life had started getting strange after I was bitten by those bugs.

By then, we'd reached town. And I realized where I wanted to go. It would be tough getting Bud to agree, but I knew I had to go there, with him or without.

Eight

THE ROOM
IS BUGGED

"Are you kidding?" Bud asked when I told him where I was going. "That would almost be like sneaking back into school."

"Come on," I said. "It'll be fun. They've got that mummy. And the fake dinosaur."

Bud shrugged. "I guess. . . ."

"Great." I headed toward the Lewington Natural History Museum. I wasn't interested in the mummy or the dinosaur right now—though they really were the coolest things in the place. I wanted to look at the bugs. And they sure had lots of those—a whole room, from what I remembered. I hadn't paid much attention the last time I was there. It was on a school trip, and our teacher kept talking the whole time, telling us all about what we were looking at.

But right now, I needed to know about bugs. I kept thinking about what that nerd had said in his report. Some bugs stick eggs in other bugs. I sure hoped those things that bit me hadn't done something like that. Or filled me with poison. I knew there were some kids who can get real sick from one bee sting. I had to find out what kind of bug had bitten me.

"The mummy's this way," Bud said when we walked into the museum. He turned toward the left.

"Go ahead," I called after him. "I want to check out something over here." I went down the hall to the right. At the end of the hallway, there was a room with a sign over the top: OUR INSECT FRIENDS.

Speaking of insects who aren't friends, the first thing I saw when I stepped inside was the nerd himself.

He looked at me and gasped, then glanced all around like he was trying to find a way to escape. What did he think? I was going to beat him up for no reason? That made me so angry, I thought about hitting him.

"You got a problem?" I asked.

He shook his head and swallowed so hard, I could hear the sound from all the way across the room.

I decided to ignore him. I started looking at the bugs. The room had glass tanks in the walls with live bugs, and they had a couple big tables in the middle of the room with tons of different dead bugs under sheets of glass. Each bug had a label. And there were some displays with pictures. One showed how a flea could jump real far. Another explained how an ant was real strong. One photo showed how a fly would eat its food by drooling on it first. Yuck. That was gross.

There must have been a couple thousand bugs altogether. But I didn't see a single one like the ones that had been chomping on me yesterday. I checked the whole place twice, just to make sure. As I was finishing up, I saw that the nerd was still in the room, studying this tank full of ants and writing stuff in a notebook.

Maybe he knew what kind of bug it was that bit me. Heck, he knew something about everything. I hated to talk to him. I wasn't even sure I could describe the bug all that well. Not with words. But maybe it was worth a try. Before I could make up my mind, Bud came into the room. "Hey, there you are," he said, running up to me.

The sight of the two of us in one place must have been too much for the nerd. He dashed out the door. Bud ignored him and told me, "I got tired of looking at the mummy. Let's go."

"Sure. Might as well." I followed Bud toward the exit from the bug room.

As we were walking out, he glanced over at one of

the tables, then said, "Hey, check this out. It looks just like the bug that bit you."

I couldn't believe he'd found it just like that. I could have slugged him. Or hugged him. "Let me see." I ran over to the display and looked where he was pointing. Yup. It was just like the ones in the cereal box, except it wasn't green. I read the label. MIMIC BEETLE.

"What's a mimic?" I asked Bud.

He shrugged. "Isn't that one of those clown guys? You know, they do stuff without talking. That's it, I think."

I was pretty sure Bud was wrong. He wasn't the greatest when it came to knowing what a word meant. I mean, I wasn't the greatest at that, either, but I was better than Bud. I figured it really didn't matter.

Under the name, the card just said, "A harmless ephemeral insect common to temperate regions of the northern hemisphere." The *harmless* part was good. I didn't care about the rest.

"Let's go," I said.

We left the museum. I was happy to be in the sun again. The light felt wonderful. I couldn't think of anywhere else to go, and neither could Bud, so we headed toward home.

I'd had so many strange things happen so far that I almost didn't notice the strangest. We were just a couple blocks away from home when I finally figured out what was wrong.

Nine

SEEING RED

"Look," I told Bud, pointing to a car in the driveway to my right. "Mr. Jenkins painted his Mustang."

"What are you talking about?" Bud asked.

"He painted it," I said again. The car used to be bright red. Now it was gray. That was a strange color for a fast car.

Bud just shook his head. I couldn't figure out what was wrong with him. I looked away from the car. Across the street, in Mrs. Pitchell's front yard, a whole bunch of flowers were blooming. Yellow ones, and blue ones, and tons of gray ones.

Gray?

I shook my head hard and looked away. The sky was

blue. That was fine. The trees were green. But there wasn't any red. No matter where I looked.

Thwack!

"Stop standing there, and let's get home," Bud said.

I followed him, trying to figure out what was going on. What if the rest of the colors went away? I didn't want to end up in a gray world. Then what if the gray went away, too?

"Hi, Lud. Hi, Bud," Mom said when we walked into the kitchen. "I made your favorite again."

"Thanks." I looked at the steaming roast, fresh out of the oven, and felt sick. But something in the kitchen smelled wonderful. I walked across the floor to the garbage can. It was filled with rotten fruit. Yellow and gray peaches. A couple gray strawberries. A hunk of watermelon, green on the outside, light gray inside. Small flies buzzed around the top of the can.

"Oh, would you take that outside for me?" Mom asked. "I cleaned out the fridge today."

"Sure." I pulled the bag out of the can and headed to the side of the house where we keep the big cans. I couldn't believe how great the fruit smelled. But it looked awful.

Fighting the urge to take a bite of one of the peaches, I tossed out the bag and went back inside. Everyone else was already at the table.

"I don't feel hungry," I said.

"Are you sick?" Mom asked.

I shook my head. "No. I had a big lunch. I think I'll skip dinner."

"You know, dinner is the most important meal of the evening," Dad said.

"I know," I told him. "But I'm just not hungry."

Mom looked at me with that *Are you getting sick?* look. I tried to look back at her with that *I'm fine* look.

"Maybe you'll be hungry later," she said.

"Maybe." I went up to the room. I might be slow to think up stuff in school, but even I knew that something strange was happening to me. I stared at my face in the mirror. My eyes looked different. Hey—that was kind of a joke. But they really did look different. They were darker. And the colored part was bigger. I picked up my toothbrush. It wasn't red anymore. It was gray. I took off my shirt and checked out the bug bites. They were fine. Not puffy or anything. There sure were a bunch of them, though. All over my chest.

But they seemed to be healing.

I went back to my room.

Pit came running in a minute later, waving an action figure in my face. "Captain Spazmodic saves the universe!" he shouted.

"That's great," I told him.

"Want to play?" he asked.

I almost said no. I wasn't feeling real good. But

playing wouldn't make me feel any worse. And I hated to let Pit down. "Sure. Let's play."

So we sat and played for a while, saving the universe. Pit was lucky. Life was simple for him. At least, right now it was. He just had kindergarten to deal with.

"Lud," Pit said when he was getting up to leave.

"What?"

"Danny Milliken called me stupid today."

"Don't you listen to him," I said. I took his arm and pulled him onto my lap. "That's going to happen. People who call names. They're the stupid ones. You remember that. Okay?"

Pit nodded. "Okay."

"And remember something else. What do I always tell you?"

"Mellons stick together," he said.

"That's right. No matter what. No matter who calls you names, or who makes fun of you, you've got Mom and Dad and me and everyone else in the family."

"Yeah." He smiled.

"Now, go to bed before May starts shouting."

He nodded and climbed off my lap. Then he laughed and pointed at my shirt.

"What?" I asked.

"You're drooling," he said. He threw his head back and laughed even louder.

"Thanks for letting me know." I wiped my chin. It was soaked.

"*Piiiiiittttt!*" May hollered from downstairs. "Bed tiiiimmme!"

I watched him race out of the room. Maybe it wasn't any easier in kindergarten. Maybe it's never easy.

I got up from the floor. It was still early. I can stay up later than Pit. But I was feeling really tired. And worried. Especially about not seeing red. And about all the drooling. It was bad enough being big and stupid. It would be awful to be all slobbery on top of that. People who don't care either way about sweat can get all funny about a little bit of spit. That's a fact.

Right now, all I could do was get ready for bed. Maybe I could figure out something tomorrow. Or better yet, maybe I'd wake up and be all normal, like when you go to sleep sick but in the morning your fever is all gone. That's the best kind of problem—the kind that goes away all by itself.

But I didn't get better while I was asleep. I got buggier. A whole lot buggier.

Ten

EAT PLENTY
OF GREENS

I woke up early again. Bud was still snoring away. At least this time I wasn't hanging from the ceiling. As I sat up on the edge of the bed and stretched, I noticed there were dark things all over my pajama top.

"What the heck?"

I reached down and tried to brush one off. It was like a thin spike, about as thick as the tube inside those clear pens. The spike didn't brush off. I pulled at one, but it wouldn't pull out, either. When I pulled, I felt this strange tugging at my chest.

I didn't like that feeling at all. I yanked off my top. Oh man. The things were stuck on me. No. It was even worse: They were growing out of me. I ran to the bathroom and looked in the mirror.

All over my chest, on my arms, too, I had them. Wherever I had a bite, a thick hair or two was sticking up. I touched the tip of one. It was springy, but kind of sharp, too. Then I felt my chest. The skin around the hair had turned hard, like plastic. I tapped it with a fingernail, and it made this clicking sound.

Man. I didn't want anyone to see that. They'd think I was some kind of freak. There's a kid in school with a bunch of pimples on his forehead, and everyone makes fun of him. I can imagine what they'd do to me.

Someone was walking down the hall. It sounded like Dad. I slammed the bathroom door shut and grabbed a shirt from the laundry basket on the floor. It didn't help. The hairs stuck right out through the shirt.

Oh man. I reached under the shirt and tried to smooth the hairs down. They sprang right back up.

I looked around the bathroom. I saw Dad's razor. But the thought of cutting the hairs made me shiver. I was afraid it would hurt. Worse, I was afraid what might drip out of them if I cut them. Maybe some kind of green goo.

There had to be something I could do. Dad's hair gel! That was it. I grabbed the jar and scooped up a big handful, then reached under my shirt and tried again. This time, the hairs stayed. After I'd slicked down the hairs on my chest, I took care of the ones on my arms.

I opened the door and walked into the hall, going past Dad.

He looked at me and sniffed. "You smell nice," he said.

Oh man. I'd forgotten that Dad's hair gel smelled. I just couldn't win. If I kept it on, I'd smell like a barbershop. If I washed it off, I'd be walking around with hairs sticking out all over my chest, looking like a porcupine or a cactus person.

I went down to breakfast.

"You smell nice," Mom said. She smiled.

Pit shook his head. "You stink," he said. He pinched his nose.

I checked my shirt, making sure none of the hairs had popped back up. Now I really didn't feel like eating. "I got to get to school early," I said. I stood up from the table and headed for the door.

It felt strange walking to school by myself. I was so used to going everywhere with Bud. But I just had to get away. It was still early, and there was nobody in the yard when I got there. I walked around back. There was this spot off on the side where each class plants a tree when they graduate. They'd been doing it since the school was built thirty years ago, so some of the trees are pretty big. I went over there and leaned against a tree. According to the sign, it had been planted ten years ago.

I stood for a while, trying to figure out what to do. The voice startled me.

"Lud, stop that. You're killing the tree."

I looked up. It was Dawn. She pointed at my hand. I hadn't realized I was holding a handful of fresh, green leaves. Worse, when I tried to say something, I realized my mouth was full. I spat out a hunk of half-chewed leaves.

"You are so gross," she said.

"But . . ." I looked at the tree. Two of the lower branches were bare. All the leaves were gone. My stomach felt full, like I'd just stuffed myself with three or four hot dogs. Oh man, I'd been eating leaves. And I didn't even know what I was doing. It was like when you get going on a bag of chips and eat them without thinking about it. Once, I watched Bud eat a whole bag of oatmeal-raisin cookies while he was watching television. I don't think he even tasted them. But this wasn't chips or cookies. It was leaves.

Then Dawn smiled and said, "But I'll say one thing for you—you smell nice."

"Thanks."

"Just take it easy on the trees." She walked off. I looked around. There still wasn't anyone in the yard. Dawn must have come early to work on a project. At least nobody else had seen me.

There was no question. I needed help. But there

wasn't anybody in my family who could help me. If it was a problem with a machine, I could ask Dad. If it was a problem with regular kid stuff, I could ask Mom. But this wasn't something a mom or dad would know about.

I didn't have a choice. There was only one person smart enough to help me. Except I wasn't sure I could show him my problem without scaring him to death.

Eleven

SHOW AND TELL

I had to talk to the nerd. *When you need a screwdriver, don't try to do the job with a fork.* That's what Dad says. I walked out to the front of the school and waited. Finally, I saw him coming down the street with his show-off friend, Sebastian. I headed toward them, wondering how I could get the nerd alone so I could talk with him.

But as soon as they spotted me, they turned off and dashed for the back door of the school. By the time I got there, they'd gone inside.

Then the bell rang, so I went in, too. I started searching the halls. I knew I'd catch up with the nerd in my first class, but I wanted to talk to him right away.

"Hey, wait up."

I looked over my shoulder. It was Bud. "Not now," I said.

"Why'd you run off?" he asked.

"I'll tell you later."

The bell rang. I rushed into class. The nerd was already at his seat. I headed toward him.

"Okay, everyone," Mr. Phermat said. "Let's get settled. Take your seats. There'll be no talking during the test."

Oh man. I sat down and tried to get the nerd's attention. He didn't even look my way. He seemed happy to be taking a test.

It would have to wait until the end of class. I looked at the test. Man. There weren't even any airplane problems. It was all trains and cars and stuff. I'd bet Mr. Phermat did it that way just to make sure I'd flunk.

I'd show him. I got out my pencil and tried my best. But it was no use. The problems didn't make any more sense than they ever did. Worst of all, I was trying so hard, I didn't even hear the bell. The next thing I knew, Mr. Phermat was standing at my desk, taking my test paper from me. I looked around. The nerd had already gone. He'd probably been the first one to hand in his test.

I left the class and checked the hall. The nerd was far ahead. He stopped at the end of the hall and looked around. Then he ducked into the boys' room. Perfect.

I'd finally be able to talk to him. I went down the hall and followed him in. By then, he was at the sink, washing his hands. A blast of hot air hit me. The radiator was stuck, so it was on all year round.

As the door closed behind me, the nerd glanced over. His eyes locked on me for a second with a look of so much fear that I laughed. I couldn't help it. He turned his head away.

I walked over to him. He tried to dash past me.

"Not so fast," I said, putting out a hand to block him.

He leaped back, his eyes darting around the room. Then he started talking to himself. "I knew I should have waited until I got home. It was only three more hours. I knew it. I could have waited."

"Stop babbling," I said.

"Yeah. Absolutely. No more babbling." He nodded, then jammed his hand in his right front pocket and pulled out a bunch of change. "Here, that's my lunch money. Take it. If it's not enough, I'll get more."

"I don't want your money," I said.

"Homework?" he asked, holding up his notebook. "It would never pass as yours, but you're welcome to it."

"No." I smacked the notebook out of his hand. "I don't want your stupid homework."

He scrunched his eyes real tight. "Just make it quick. Okay? Alacrity would be appreciated. Get it over with.

73

Don't break my glasses. Mom really hates when that happens."

"I'm not going to hurt you!" I yelled. Though it was going to be a hard promise to keep.

He opened one eye. "Then what is the purpose of this encounter?"

"Help me," I said.

"With what?"

I reached down and pulled up the front of my shirt.

He screamed and leaped away like a human cricket. I thought he was going to jump through the little window at the back wall—the thick frosted one. But instead, his face changed. All of a sudden, he turned from a cricket to an owl.

"Chitinous exoskeletal material extruding cilia . . . ," he said, taking a step toward me. He reached out a hand and said, "May I?"

"Yeah. Sure."

He lifted one of the hairs, poked at my chest, and said a bunch more stuff.

"What are you talking about?" I didn't understand any of what he'd said.

He explained, but it was just another jumble of big words. I don't think even most adults would have understood him. I waited for a sentence to pass by that I recognized as English. No such luck until finally, he said, "You appear to be taking on some of the attributes of an insect."

"You don't look surprised," I said.

"I've encountered numerous strange events," he told me. "The density of phenomena in this vicinity is staggering."

I had no idea what that meant, either, but at least he seemed interested. "So, can you help me?" I asked.

He grinned, and for the first time in my life, I felt scared of a little nerd. "I'd love to try."

"So let's go," I said.

"Now?" He tore his eyes away from my insect body and looked up to my face. "Not while school's on. I can't skip school."

"But—"

"Meet me out front after school," he said. As he walked away, he looked back and said, "You know, you really smell nice." Then he dashed out of the bathroom, spewing a trail of large words behind him.

I was about to leave when I found that I had another problem.

Twelve

SLIPPING THROUGH
THE CRACKS

More hairs had started growing on my arms. Lots
more. I couldn't go through the school day like that. I
turned my head to look at my face in the mirror.

Oh man.

No way. For a minute, I froze. I just couldn't believe
what I saw. But it was real. I'd turned my head around
without turning my body. Whoa. I didn't like that at
all. I turned my head back around, then carefully turned
my whole body. I checked the mirror. I was drooling so
bad, I looked like some kind of stuck water fountain.
Between the hairs and the spit, there was no way I
wanted people staring at me. I had to get out. I figured
I could hang around somewhere nearby and wait for
the nerd. I'd get in trouble later for cutting class, but

that kind of trouble was nothing. Not when you looked at what I was going through right now.

I peeked past the bathroom door to make sure nobody was in the hall, then slipped out.

Next thing I knew, I heard footsteps coming toward me. I ran down the hall the other way and headed for the gym. There was another door at the side of the gym, next to the bleachers.

Oh man. It was locked. I was doomed. The steps were following me. Teachers are like bloodhounds. Once they think there's someone they can catch, they never stop chasing. I looked at the bottom of the door and saw a gap. At least half an inch.

Bugs could get in and out of just about anywhere. I'd seen it a million times. Bugs and hamsters. Bud and I had pet hamsters once. They got right out of their cage. I saw them slip under the opening—flat as a stomped soda can.

The footsteps came closer. I had to try. I dropped on my stomach and pushed my head against the bottom of the door. I halfway hoped it wouldn't work. Because if I could do it, that meant I was a lot less normal than I wanted to be. As I pushed, I felt something flattening in my head. It was like my skull was made of plastic. Man. It was weird. I closed my eyes and pushed harder. Even with my eyes closed, I could tell my head wasn't in the gym anymore. Everything was brighter. I opened one eye. My head had made it through the crack under the door. I kept pushing. I got my arms through. I didn't want to look back, but I couldn't help myself.

I wish I hadn't. It was like my body was cut in half. My chest was partway through, but it disappeared under the door. I pulled the rest of myself through real fast before I could think too much about everything inside me squishing down. I didn't see how it could be very healthy. But at least I'd gotten out of the building.

As I slid my feet out through the crack, my sneakers got stuck. I had to twist around and yank real hard. At first, that didn't work. But I gave a super-hard tug, and they popped through. I heard footsteps on the gym floor. Then someone rattled the locked door.

I'd just made it.

Hey, I thought of a joke. How fast did I get out of the school? I got out in nothing flat. That's a good one. But there's no way I could explain it to anybody. What could I say? I was trapped in a room and then I got out by flattening myself. So I got out in nothing flat.

At least I was free. Now I just had to wait until the nerd got out of school.

As I walked around the side of the school, I saw Charlie, the custodian, talking to another guy. They were standing by the trees. Charlie grabbed one of the bare branches, where I'd eaten the leaves. I heard

the other guy say, "No problem. I'll be back to spray tomorrow."

The guy walked to a truck. On the side, it said, BUG-B-GONE EXTERMINATORS. There was a picture of a dead bug painted under the name. Somehow, it made me feel sad.

I waited until Charlie left, then snuck back as far as I could between the trees, figuring I could hang out there until school ended.

Overhead, a plane rumbled. I looked up at it and I knew how fast it was going. I knew which direction it was headed.

I thought about how I'd slipped under the door. And about how I'd turned my head halfway around. I wondered what else I could do. I tried to remember what I'd seen at the museum. There were all those pictures of what bugs could do. They could jump real far and pick up heavy stuff.

Might as well try, I thought. I jumped. Whoa. Unbelievable. I shot up about ten feet. Too bad I didn't like to play basketball. When I landed, I looked around for something to lift. I didn't see any rocks. I saw a bug. A big one. Ms. Clevis's shiny blue Volkswagen Beetle. I snuck over to the parking lot and grabbed the back bumper.

I pulled up, and the rear wheels left the ground. Wow. I put it down gently. As I walked back to the trees, feeling good about how strong I was, I realized something that took the nice feeling right out of me. I'd been strong all my life. It didn't do me any good. It didn't make people like me or want to be with me. It just made them afraid. Now I was even stronger. But it wouldn't make any difference. Either way, I was just some sort of monster to them.

I hid beneath the trees and waited for school to get out.

Thirteen

HOME OF THE NERD

When the bell rang, I watched everybody leave the building. Bud came out right away and stood by the front door. He kept looking around. I guess he was waiting for me. That made me feel good. But I watched as everyone else walked around him. They all made sure not to get too close. Man. I'd been in the middle of it all my life, but it was even worse, seeing it from over by the trees. Nobody wanted anything to do with Bud.

I had an urge to go over, just so he wouldn't be alone. But I didn't want any of my teachers to spot me. Or any of the kids. Not with all these hairs sticking out of me. I felt real bad leaving him out there, especially since I knew he was waiting for me. And since I knew I wasn't going to show up.

"Ready?"

The voice made me jump. Not a good thing, since I was under a big branch.

"Ouch!" I shouted as the branch smacked against my head. I rubbed the spot.

"Didn't mean to scare you," the nerd said.

"You didn't scare me," I told him. "Nothing scares me. You just surprised me. How'd you know I'd be here?"

This big smile stretched across his face. "Where else would you be?" he asked.

I wasn't sure what he meant, so I let it drop.

He pointed to the tree next to me. "You'd better cut that out," he said.

I looked over. Three or four of the branches were bare. I rubbed my tongue around in my mouth. Oh yuck. I'd been snacking again. "I didn't know I was doing it," I said.

He nodded. "Instinctive behavior. This is fascinating. Come on. Let's go to my house. We can cut behind the school and avoid detection."

I followed him, looking back to see if Bud was still there.

"Holy cow! Cut that out!" he shouted.

"What?" I asked.

"Turn your head back around," he told me.

"Oh." I'd forgotten I could do that.

"And here," he said, holding out a handful of paper towels. "You might want to wipe your chin."

"Thanks."

As we reached the street behind the school yard, he dug his hand into his pocket and pulled out a pen. "What color is this?" he asked, pushing it toward my face.

"Gray," I told him.

"Outstanding," he said. "I suspected as much. Insect vision is spectrally shifted. You can't discern the low frequencies, but you have great acuity for the ultra-violet."

My hand shot out and grabbed him by the shirt-sleeve. It was so fast, I didn't even see my arm move.

"Superior reflexes," he said.

I didn't mean to grab him, but I had to get one thing straightened out. "Talk so I can understand you."

He opened his mouth. I think he was about to say some kind of put-down. That would have been a big mistake. He was my only hope, but I wasn't going to let him make fun of me. Finally, he said, "I'll endeavor— sorry, I'll try to limit my vocab—I mean, my choice of words."

I let my hand drop. "Thanks, nerd."

"My name's Norman," he said.

"Thanks, Norman. You were talking about seeing red stuff, right?"

"Right. Insects can't see some colors that we can. But they can see some that we can't." He looked at me like he was waiting to see if I understood.

I nodded.

For most of the rest of the walk, I didn't say anything. But there was one thing I had to know. As we reached his house, I asked him, "Why are you helping me?"

He shrugged. "How often do I get a chance to help anyone? I can't hit a baseball. I can't sink a basket or kick a goal. I fall off my bike so often, the sides of my seat are scuffed. But there's one thing I'm good at. And that's science. If anyone can help you, I can. There's no way I can walk away from a challenge like that. Even if you did beat me up seventeen times since kindergarten."

"Seventeen?" I asked. I couldn't even remember beating him up before. "Are you sure?"

He pointed to the side of his glasses, where the frame was taped together. "Last December."

"Sorry."

Then he bent over and pulled up his left pants leg. "First grade," he said, pointing to a scar on his shin. He mentioned a couple other times when I'd done something to him, including the other day when I'd knocked him down by the lockers.

Now I felt bad. I guess it made sense that he'd remember getting hurt more than I'd remember hurting him. But I couldn't believe I'd been that rotten to him.

I couldn't believe he was being this nice, either. "And you're still going to help me?" I asked.

"Yup."

I didn't know what to say.

"Don't worry about it." He waved at the door ahead of us. "Let's get started."

I followed him inside and up to his room. Man. The place was just like the museum, only smaller. There were jars and bottles all over the room, and rocks and posters and hundreds of books. "This place reminds me of school," I said.

"Thanks. Now, lift your shirt," he said.

I pulled up my shirt and stood there while he stared at me and made the kind of sounds someone makes when he's thinking real hard. "Unfortunately, it seems to be progressing," he said. Then he jumped back from me and said, "I mean, it's spreading."

I looked down. I did seem to have more of the hairs poking through my skin. And the hard patches looked wider. "Can you stop it?"

"Tell me everything that's happened."

I told him about the cereal box and the bugs and the barrel of green goo. I told him about the museum. When I mentioned the mimic beetle, his face got a funny expression for a second, but he didn't say anything.

"What's wrong?" I asked.

"Mimic beetles copy other insects. So, maybe that's

what you're doing. And if you looked at all the insects in the museum, maybe you're copying all of them. I suspect the green liquid had an effect on the beetles that bit you, also. First, we have to figure out what's going on. There had to be some kind of mutation involved. But it's too soon to really make any guesses." He grabbed a camera from a shelf over his desk. "We can keep track of the spread this way." He clicked a picture.

"How?"

"In an hour, I'll take another picture. We can compare them to see how much you've changed. Hey, I have a better idea. We can use a computer program to compare the pictures."

"You have a program to do that?" The only programs I knew about were the writing ones we used in school, and games.

"I don't have one, but it should be easy enough to write." He sat down at his computer and started typing. I didn't say anything. It looked like he was real busy. And happy. So I just sat and waited. After a while, he got up and said, "Okay. Let's get another shot."

I stood and lifted my shirt for the camera. He took the picture, then sent it to the computer. As he was doing that, I thought of a joke. I guess I was so worried about what he was doing that I didn't even realize I was talking out loud until I heard my own voice. "Aren't you worried your program will have bugs in it?"

He glanced at me with a puzzled look, then turned back to the screen. "It's definitely spreading," he said. "Okay. We've established a baseline. Now we have to determine what factors might slow the transformation and perhaps even enable us to reverse the process." He looked up at me with a grin. Then his face got a worried look and he said, "I mean, let's see if we can stop this and then make you better. Okay?"

"Great." I still couldn't believe he was helping me. Especially after he'd mentioned how often I'd hurt him.

"Follow me." He grabbed a flashlight from his desk drawer and a stack of comic books from the floor and headed down the stairs.

I followed him into a kitchen. If his room looked like it belonged in a museum, his kitchen looked like it should be in a restaurant. I saw a couple of ovens and two refrigerators. He headed for a huge metal door that was built into one wall. He pulled the handle, and the door swung open. A blast of cold air hit me in the face. "Man. That's a *big* freezer," I said.

He nodded, then handed me the flashlight and the books. "Get in," he said.

Fourteen

COLD FACTS

"What?"

"Get in," he said again. "We need to see if temperature is a factor. Hurry up. Get in. You'll skew the results if you stay at room temperature."

"Can I breathe in there?" I looked inside. There were long shelves on both sides and in the back. But unfortunately, there was plenty of room in the middle for me to stand.

"No problem. The volume of air is adequate for the time span we need. Besides, there's a handle on the inside. You won't be trapped."

I took a step inside. It felt like winter. Hey—I thought of a joke. I guess my bites would become cold cuts.

"Wait. It would be better if you removed your shirt," he said.

I just stared at him.

"Really," he said.

I pulled it off.

"You'll be fine," he told me. "Promise." He closed the door.

It got as dark as it could get. The dark hit me so fast, I didn't even notice the cold right away. For a second, I felt myself getting real worried. Then I had trouble turning on the flashlight because my fingers were stiff.

I had to be crazy, trusting the nerd. Well, at least I had comic books. I stood there and started reading. It seemed like I was in there forever. Finally, he opened the door back up.

"You got a big family?" I asked as I followed him back up the stairs.

"No. Just me, Mom, and Dad," he said.

"Why the giant freezer?"

"Oh. Mom's a caterer. She makes food for all kinds of parties and banquets and stuff. She's always cooking."

"Sounds like my mom," I said. "She cooks tons of stuff every day, but just for the family."

Back in his room, he took another picture. Then he put it in the computer.

"Okay," he said after he'd hit a couple of keys and

slid the mouse around. "Good news. As I'd expected, a cold environment slows the rate of change. Now we have to see about heat."

"You aren't going to chuck me in the oven, are you?" I thought about the big ovens in the kitchen.

He shook his head. "No. This will be localized. I suspect heat accelerates the process. So we'll minimize the area."

He ran off. I didn't bother asking him what he meant. He came back a minute later with a hair dryer. He switched it on and pointed it at my chest. The warm air felt great to me after I'd been in that freezer. But as we watched, the shiny black tips of more hairs popped through my skin where the hair dryer was blowing on it.

"Heat is bad," he said, switching off the dryer. "I better take some skin samples." He reached into his desk and pulled out a wooden box. Inside, he had a bunch of glass slides, like the kind you use with a microscope, and a couple small knives.

He took out a knife and moved it toward my chest.

Next thing I knew, my hand was clamped on his wrist.

"Ow! Come on. I'm just going to scrape a small sample. It won't hurt. Honest."

I let go and he yanked his hand back. Then he reached forward again.

"Ouch. You're breaking my wrist."

I looked down. I'd grabbed him again. I'd done it without thinking. I mean, my teachers were always yelling about how I never thought about what I did, but this was different. I really didn't think about grabbing his hand. It was the same as when I'd been eating the leaves. My hand acted like it had a brain of its own, and it didn't bother telling my brain what it was planning to do. I let go.

"Look, just close your eyes for a second. Okay?" He stepped away from me. "You've got insect reflexes. You'll defend yourself against any attack you can see coming."

"Yeah. Sure." I closed my eyes and waited, wondering how much it would hurt.

"Ouccchhhh! Let go!"

I opened my eyes. I'd locked my fingers around his wrist. "How'd I do that?"

"Other sense organs," he said. "Those hairs can probably detect motion. Look, we don't have time to investigate all of this." He handed me the knife. "Here. You do it. Just scrape off a little bit."

I wiped away the hair goo on a small spot, then took the knife and scraped it over the hard stuff on my chest. It didn't hurt. I got a little on the tip of the knife and handed it to him.

"Now what?" I asked.

"I need a little time to think about this and do some research," he told me.

"Can you help me?"

"I hope so," he said.

"Thanks." I looked down at my chest. My body didn't seem all that human anymore. I tried to look into my mind, to see if it was human. As far as I could tell, it hadn't changed. But I'd never really spent any time trying to look at my own mind.

"I'll talk to you tomorrow," he said. He reached out his hand toward me.

My own hand shot out.

"Ouch! My wrist. I just wanted to shake hands."

"Sorry." I let go. Man, these reflexes were fast. I thanked him again, put my shirt on, then headed downstairs and out of the house.

Bud was standing on the sidewalk.

Fifteen

TROUBLE BY
THE YARD

"What were you doing in there?" he asked, looking hurt.

"The nerd—I mean Norman—was helping me with something," I told him.

"I shouldn't even talk to you," he said. "Running off without me. I shouldn't have bothered following you. I've been waiting out here for hours."

"Sorry. But I really needed his help."

"What with?" he asked.

"I'm turning into a bug," I told him. "Those bugs that bit me—you know, in the cereal box. They're mimic beetles. That means they copy other things. So, with them biting me, that must mean I'm copying them. Or maybe I'm copying all kinds of bugs. I didn't really understand that part. But the green goo made them change."

"So you think you're a bug," Bud said.

"Yeah. I mean, I know I am." It felt good to share my problem with him.

Bud laughed. "Is this part of your act for the talent show? It's pretty good. Bugs are funny. Tell me some more."

"No. I'm serious. I'm a bug." I pulled up the front of my shirt. "Look. Bug hairs."

Bud grinned. "Man. That is a good one. You'll be a real hit at the show." He slapped me on the back and laughed some more.

I gave up trying to convince him. But I had a funny feeling that sooner or later, he'd believe me. Unless Norman could figure out how to help me change back.

We walked a bit more—then Bud said, "Just don't go running off somewhere without me again. Okay? It doesn't feel good to get ditched like that."

"Okay. Sorry."

"No problem."

Thwack! He smacked me on the back of the head. I wondered why I didn't grab his arm like I'd done with Norman. Maybe because he was my brother. That made sense. Like how an ant won't attack another ant from the same hill. I'd seen that on TV.

"Let's cut over this way," Bud said, pointing to Mr.

Terranova's house. We were a couple blocks away from home, but we could get right there by going across Mr. Terranova's yard and then up the hill behind our house.

"Sure." That wasn't a problem. He was a friend of my dad's and he didn't care if we walked on his property. I just didn't want to run into him, because he liked to talk. I mean, he liked to talk a whole lot, and he never talked about anything interesting. So I checked the porch to make sure he wasn't there. Then I followed Bud.

The first couple of steps, I didn't notice anything wrong. But about halfway along the front yard, I started to feel wobbly. Then I stopped right where I was.

"Oh no," I said when I noticed what was at the edge of the lawn.

"What's wrong?" Bud asked.

I stared at the little paper flag on the stick. I knew what it was. That's what they put on a yard after it's been sprayed. There was stuff on the lawn to kill the weeds. And to kill bugs.

Wow. I felt really dizzy. I took a step backwards. I knew I had to get off the grass fast.

"Hey, look who's here," Mr. Terranova said, pushing open his screen door and stepping onto the porch. "I thought I heard voices."

"Hi," Bud said.

I waved at him and backed up another step. "Hi."

"Don't run off, youngster," he said. "You know I like to chat."

"Uh, yeah." I took another step backwards. But the lawn spray was getting to me. I couldn't stand up. All of a sudden, I fell to my knees.

"Yup," Mr. Terranova said. "Sure is nice to have a lawn like this. Takes a lot of work, but it's worth it. Go ahead. Roll around if you want. Enjoy it."

"Thanks," I said weakly. I started to put my hand down so I could push myself back to my feet. But I realized if I touched the grass with my bare skin, I'd be in even bigger trouble. If just the smell was making me this dizzy, I was afraid to think what would happen if I got the stuff on my skin. So I tried to rock myself up to my feet.

That turned out to be a real bad idea. I lost my balance and fell on my back.

"How about you, Bud?" Mr. Terranova asked. "Don't you want to join your brother? When I was a lad, I loved to roll in the grass. That was before we had all these fancy lawn mowers and riding tractors. Had to push the mowers when I was a boy. Yessiree, push 'em by hand. Let me tell you, that was hard work. Go ahead, boy. Roll around."

"No thanks." Bud stared at me like I was crazy, lying there in the grass on my back.

"Help me," I whispered, hoping that for once in his life, Bud would use his brain.

"What?" Bud asked. "I can't hear you when you whisper."

"What's that?" Mr. Terranova asked. He turned his left ear toward Bud. "Speak up. I can't hear either of you."

I reached out and grabbed the cuff of Bud's pants. I barely had enough strength to close my fingers.

"Stop that, Lud," he said, yanking his leg from my grip.

I tried to say something else, but everything got real fuzzy. Then everything faded away.

Next thing I knew, I was getting hit in the face with a hard stream of water. "Cut it out!"

"You okay now?" Bud asked. He was standing there with a hose.

I looked around. We were on the side of our house, next to the driveway. "How'd I get here?"

"I carried you," Bud said. "It was like that time when you ran headfirst into the side of the house. Knocked you right out. I figured I'd better bring you home." He looked over his shoulder. "Oh gross—you drooled all over my shirt, too."

"Sorry."

"That's okay. I'm drier than you." He laughed and sprayed me with the hose again.

"Stop that."

Bud turned off the nozzle. "Hey, you better wipe yourself off before we go inside. If you get the floor wet, Mom will be real steamed."

He was right. So I dried off. But when we got inside, I found out that someone was real angry anyhow. And it wasn't Mom.

Sixteen

WHAT WOOD
YOU CHEW?

The minute I stepped inside, I could hear Dad shouting from upstairs. "Those darn termites! That does it. Lud, get up here. I need you."

"Sounds like work," Bud said. "Think I'll go back outside." He dashed out the door.

That was okay. I didn't mind helping Dad. "What's wrong?" I asked when I got to the top of the stairs.

"Look at this." He pointed at the door to my room. He was so angry, his hand was shaking.

"Oh no." I looked at the bottom. The wood was all chewed up, like something was eating at it. Man—I knew what had chewed the wood. Me.

"Termites!" Dad said. "I'm gonna get them once and for all. Go grab the sprayer."

I went up to the attic and got Dad's spray can. I figured I'd have to slip out of the house before he started spraying, or I'd be in big trouble. "Maybe you should hold off," I told him.

"Why? So they can eat up the rest of the house? Darn bugs."

I couldn't answer him. What could I say? *Guess what, Dad? Your son's a bug. A real big bug.* I couldn't ever tell him that. He'd go crazy. I could just see him turning the spray on me. I started to walk away.

"Where you going?" he asked.

"Outside." I figured I could hang out in the yard until the air cleared. I was still a little dizzy from Mr. Terranova's lawn.

"Stay here," Dad said. "I need you to work the pump. Got to get two men on this. You pump hard and I'll spray. Hit 'em with full pressure, really get the stuff into every crack. We're going to wipe out every single insect in this house."

It felt good that he thought of me as a man. It felt bad that I was about to end up in a cloud of bug-killer spray. Maybe I could stay out of the way if I kept behind him. I started pumping. Dad lifted the hose and pointed the nozzle at the floor, next to the door. "Die, bugs." He pulled the trigger.

Nothing happened.

"Darn. Let me see that." He grabbed the can and

shook it. "Empty." He looked at his watch. "The store's closed. Don't worry. I'll get some more spray first thing in the morning."

I put the sprayer back in the attic. Man, it was hot up there. I hurried out. I didn't want to be changing into a bug any faster than I had to.

I went downstairs. Dad was in the kitchen. "Maybe it's not termites," I said.

"Doesn't matter what kind of bug it is," he said. "I'm going to get the good stuff. It'll kill anything that wiggles, crawls, or flies. Big or small, kills 'em all." He grinned.

"Great." I went out back. Bud was playing monster ape again, knocking over stuff, but I didn't feel like joining him. I didn't feel like doing anything. So I just sat and watched him. He was lucky. Tomorrow, he'd be pretty much the same as he was today. And the same the next day. I didn't know what was going to happen to me. But I knew one thing: After everyone went to sleep, I was going to fix the sprayer so it wouldn't work. Hey, that was almost a joke. I'd said I'd fix it so it wouldn't work. But if it were fixed, it would work.

Even my jokes didn't cheer me up right then.

I walked over to one of the washing machines. I'd seen the bugs run under it the other day. Maybe they were still there. I didn't want to get bit again, but I figured it wouldn't hurt to get a closer look at them. I flipped over the machine.

There were plenty of bugs underneath. Except they weren't moving. My stomach twisted around when I looked at them. They were all dead.

A breeze came through the yard and scattered the dried-out bodies. Just like that, they were gone. I should have felt glad about them being dead, since they'd done this to me. But I didn't. I felt sorry for them.

When we went in for dinner, I forced down some food to make Mom happy. At bedtime, I waited until it sounded like everybody was asleep. We Mellons aren't the quietest sleepers in the world. Sometimes my parents' room sounds like a place where people test out chain saws. And May whistles through her nose when she sleeps. It's almost like she's playing a flute. Badly.

I went into the hall and up to the attic. I didn't want to turn on a light, so I felt my way around. I kept one hand on the door so I wouldn't get trapped, and reached around for the can.

That's when something dropped onto my hand. It must have been a spider. I jumped. Bad move, since the ceiling was pretty low in the attic. I smacked the top of my head so hard, it felt like someone had set off a firecracker inside my brain. For the second time in one day, everything went black.

The last thought I had as I passed out was how hot it felt. Real hot. Like an oven.

Seventeen

TOTALLY BUGGY

Oh man. It took me a minute to remember where I was. I sat up and felt my head for a bump.

Something was wrong.

Please. Let it be a dream.

My whole head was covered with stiff, pointy hairs. So was my hand. Only it wasn't a hand. It was too dark to see for sure what it had turned into. I think I was glad I couldn't see too much. But my hand ended in some kind of claw. It felt like my thumb had gotten bigger and my other four fingers had gotten stuck together.

A breeze from somewhere broke through the heat. I could feel it over my whole body. And the smell of flowers. Real strong. It was coming from outside. Mom had planted a cherry tree in the yard years ago. I could smell the blossoms. I could taste them, too. But my mouth was closed. I realized I could taste them with my arms. No joke. Where the air hit my arms, I could taste the flowers.

I stood up, making sure I didn't hit my head again. I needed to know what I'd become. There was a bulb in the middle of the attic, with a chain. I felt around for the chain, then gave it a yank.

The attic filled with light.

I'd forgotten that Dad stacked up a bunch of old mirrors against the far wall.

When I saw the reflections, I jumped.

But this time, I didn't bang my head. I spun around with my belly toward the ceiling. My hands—or whatever they were—and my feet hit the ceiling and stuck. I'd done it without thinking. Like how a cat lands on its feet. Or how a ninja in one of those karate movies leaps around. I felt strong and light. I could have hung there all day with no trouble.

I took a step, then another. The breeze was coming through the vent holes Dad had cut. I didn't even have to wonder whether I could fit through. I knew there was enough space. I crawled down the ceiling to the floor, and then slipped through the opening.

I crawled up to the roof. The sun was rising. The world filled with greens and blues and a color I had never seen before. Everything curved around from the

center to the corners of my eyes. It was hard to describe, but it was sort of like those giant movie screens that wrap around a wall. It helped me know how far away everything was.

The sun felt wonderful. My skin, or whatever it was, soaked up the heat. It made my whole body feel good.

After a while, I crawled down the side of the house. The ground felt great. I could taste the grass through my hands. I'd decided to still call them hands, even though they looked more like claws. I stood up and looked around, thinking about what I'd seen in the mirror.

The eyes. That was the strangest thing. My eyes were huge. My head was bigger, too. And I had small antennas on top of it. If tonight was Halloween, I'd be the coolest kid on the planet. But it was spring, and I was nothing but a giant bug. I didn't know what to do. I thought about going back to the bedroom and getting Bud. But what could he do for me? I wasn't smart enough to figure anything out, and I was smarter than Bud. Besides, if Dad saw me, he'd flip. And I didn't want to scare Mom. She wasn't afraid of bugs, but she'd never seen one this size. I guess nobody had.

Something else felt wrong. My pajama top was tight. I took it off, but that didn't help. I kept seeing a shape out of the corner of my eye, like when you have stuff stuck to your nose and you almost can't see it. But this was on my shoulder. No, it was over my shoulder.

I turned my head around and saw that I had wings. Big ones. After a while, when I got over the shock, I found out I could move them. When I shrugged my shoulders, the wings moved. I tried flapping them together. First just one big flap. Nothing happened. Then I tried a couple faster flaps.

Whoa.

It was like someone had grabbed me under my arms and lifted me up. Right off, I went up a foot or two.

I stopped flapping and dropped to the ground.

Okay. This could be interesting. I flapped a bit slower. This time, I didn't shoot up into the air. I went up slowly. Not bad. I flew a little higher and looked down. It was weird, seeing my feet dangling like that, not touching the ground.

So I could go up. But that wouldn't do me much good unless I could also go other ways. I wondered how I could go forward. I tried leaning, then almost toppled over. No. That wasn't the way to do it. Then I tried flapping back a little with my wings.

It worked.

Except I shot forward real fast. Right into the side of the house.

Kasplat!

I felt like a bug that had smacked a windshield. I slid to the ground.

I guess it was like driving a car. You could go places easily, but if you messed up, you got hurt. I turned away from the house and tried again. This time, I managed to fly around the yard without slamming into anything.

I flew around the yard a couple more times.

"*Luuuudddddd!* Where are you?"

Oh man. May was calling for me. I thought about just flying away. But then Mom would worry. I fluttered back to the ground and stood by the side of the house.

"I'm out here," I called. My voice sounded nearly normal. Maybe just a little bit buzzy. Hey, I thought of a joke. If my voice was kind of rough, that made me a hoarse fly. "I got up early. I'm heading out for school."

"What about breakfast?" May called.

"I ate already," I said. I looked over at the trees next to the house. Sure enough, I'd munched down on one of the branches. So I wasn't lying.

"There ain't no school," May called. "It's Saturday."

"I want to get a head start for next week," I told her.

I slipped out of the yard before May could argue with me. But I hadn't gone more than a couple steps when I heard Bud shouting, "Hey, Lud! You out there? Wait for me. Okay? Wait for me, Lud."

"I'll meet you later," I called back. Then I hurried down the street. I was only wearing my pajama bottoms, but the way I looked, that didn't really seem to matter. With luck, nobody would see me.

It's amazing how bad luck can be when you need it to be good.

Eighteen

SEE YOU

I flew above the town. At first, I followed the streets. Then I realized I didn't have to. I could go wherever I wanted, even right over houses and trees. Somehow, I knew exactly how far away everything was. I knew how long it would take to get to Norman's house, or back home, or anywhere else. Once I got the hang of it, I didn't even have to think.

This was even better than having my own airplane.

After a while, my shoulders got tired, so I came down and started walking.

That's when I ran into her.

Dawn. The last person I wanted to scare. She was coming down her porch steps, holding her collie on a leash.

She looked up. And then she screamed.

I must have scared her bad. Because Dawn isn't the kind of girl who goes off screaming for no reason. But I guess I was a whole lot of reasons.

I ran away.

Man, I could run fast, too. Before I knew it, I was blocks from her house, right by the school. I ducked back in the trees. I felt awful. I didn't want to scare anybody. I didn't want anybody screaming just because they saw me.

But that look in her eyes—the terror. I'd seen it before. I just hadn't paid too much attention to it. I'd seen it all the time in smaller kids. And every kid in school was smaller than me. Except for Bud. I'd seen that look in the nerd's—I mean, in Norman's eyes every day. And he was helping me.

Man, I really was a bug. Even back when I looked like a human, I guess I was really nothing better than a scary insect. The only difference now was that my outside matched my inside. Maybe I should just stay a lousy bug.

I was so busy thinking about all of this that I didn't pay any attention to the rumbling I felt. It was weird. I could feel the ground shaking through the hairs in my legs. I looked over and saw a truck. A couple guys jumped out of it and pulled a hose from the back. It wasn't a fire truck. It was some kind of truck with a tank.

The guys slipped masks over their heads and onto their mouths and noses.

They pointed the hose at the trees.

There was a hiss, and this big, foggy cloud sprayed out of the hose. It shot over the trees and started to sink down.

On the side of the truck, I saw the picture of the dead bug. The one on its back with its feet in the air. I looked up over my head. The fog was drifting down. All around. There was no way I could get out in time.

And I couldn't fly up. I'd go right through the spray.

If it touched me, I figured I was one dead bug.

Nineteen

CAN YOU DIG IT?

There was no time to think. Even if there was, I never was any good at thinking my way out of trouble. Norman had said I did stuff by instinct. Maybe that was my only hope. I shut my brain down—that wasn't so hard—and let my body take over.

It worked.

I dropped to the ground and started to dig. My arms were so strong and fast, I made a hole right away. I slipped into it and I kept on moving. It was easy. It sort of felt like swimming through something real thick. I just scooped out some space ahead of me and then pushed my way forward. I didn't need to make much of a hole, since I could squish through just about any small space.

It was dark, but that didn't matter. I knew exactly where I was. I moved toward Norman's house. Every inch of my body helped tell me things. There were thousands of clues. I could feel and hear stuff all around me. I knew when I was under a road. I felt the cars rolling along.

It was nice underground—cool and wet. It was tempting to close my eyes and rest. Maybe take a nap, down here safe and dark, surrounded by soil. Nice and safe. Maybe just stay here. Sleep for a while.

No. I realized I was starting to think more and more like a bug. If that happened, I might never get better. I kept digging.

Finally, I popped up from a hole in the middle of Norman's front yard. I shook the dirt off my body and climbed up the side of the house. The window was open, but there was a screen on it.

He was lying in his bed, reading.

"Hey," I called. "It's me."

He looked over. Then he jumped up and ran to the window. "Good grief. I told you to avoid hot places. What did you do, spend the night in a furnace?" He pulled off the screen and stepped back.

I crawled in. "Attic," I told him.

"Well, this pretty much verifies the heat hypothesis," he said. "Though I imagine that's much more satisfying a realization for me than it is for you."

"What do I do?" I asked.

He shook his head. "I don't know yet. But I'll figure something out."

His doorbell rang.

"Wait here," he said.

I started to sit, then decided I'd feel better off the ground. So I crawled up the wall and across the ceiling to the corner over his bed.

I heard two sets of footsteps a moment later. He came back into the room with his show-off friend, Sebastian.

"Lud," Norman said, "I brought someone who can help."

I watched as Sebastian looked around the room. "What are you talking about, Norman?" he asked. "There's nobody here. Let me guess—you have a new imaginary playmate."

I dropped down from the ceiling, landing lightly on Norman's bed.

Sebastian snapped his head toward me. He opened his mouth to scream. But no sound came out. Instead, his eyes rolled back and he fainted. Dropped right down on the floor with a thud.

"I forgot about his fear of bugs," Norman said. He looked at me. "Wait here while I get some water." He ran out, then came back a minute later with a glass of water.

Norman managed to get Sebastian to wake up. But as soon as he saw me, he fainted again. Finally, on the third try, Norman said to him, "It's just Lud. Try to deal with it."

Sebastian nodded, though I noticed he wouldn't look in my direction.

"I can see where he'll be a lot of help," I said.

"He will be," Norman said. "As flaky as he might appear, I know I can count on him in an emergency. Except for this irrational problem he has with insects, he's really pretty brave. He's been through a lot. Actually, he went through something like you did, but not quite so hairy an experience. Now, me, I was a lot hairier. Thank goodness that's over with."

I didn't know what he was talking about.

He turned back to Sebastian. "You okay now?"

Sebastian nodded. He sat up. Then Norman told him what had happened to me.

And after all that, neither of them had any idea what to do to help.

I got up and walked over to a small mirror on Norman's wall. Man, I was ugly. Big fly eyes. My jaw was all funny, like it could move sideways. I didn't seem to have a nose. And my body was just as bad, all stiff and hard and covered with those thick hairs. "Why couldn't I be a butterfly or something?" I said. "I had to be something ugly."

"That's it!" Norman shouted.

"What?" I asked.

"I have an idea. It's dangerous, but it might be your only chance. Are you willing to take a risk?"

I glanced back at the mirror. I thought about how scary and ugly I was. But I could fly. And I could dig. And I could figure out how fast a plane was going just by looking at it. For a kid who never got anything better than a C on a math test, that was something pretty cool. And if I became me again, was I any better off? People would still be scared of me. I'd be stupid and ugly, and I wouldn't be able to fly.

"I have to think about it," I told him.

"You'd better think fast," he told me.

"Why?"

"There isn't much time," he said. "Pretty soon, I suspect you won't be able to think at all."

Twenty

KEEP THE CHANGE

I didn't know what he was talking about.

"You're like a bug on the outside," he said. "But you haven't changed completely. You can still talk. And a bug can't do that. It can make sounds, but not anything resembling human speech. So I think you're still changing inside."

"That's crazy," I said. But as I spoke, I realized that my voice sounded even rougher than before. Maybe my throat was changing inside, like he said.

"Even worse, your mind is changing. Right now, you can still think. But eventually, you'll be all insect. Both your body and your mind. You probably don't even realize you're grooming yourself."

I looked at my hands. I was in the middle of licking

one, and I was running the other up and down one of my antennas.

"There's another thing," Norman said. I could tell from his voice that this was the worst news of all.

"What?"

"Mimic bugs are ephemeral," he said. An instant later, he howled—"Ouch!"—as my hand clamped on his arm. "That means—"

He stopped and looked at Sebastian.

"Tell me," I said.

"It means they don't live very long."

I thought about the dried bug bodies underneath the washing machine. "Maybe it'll be different for me," I said. "People live longer than bugs."

"I'll tell you something," Norman said. "I know what it's like to be different. You and me, we're both different. I'm smart and, let's face it, a nerd. You're big and scary and kind of rough. But you know what?"

"What?" I asked.

"As long as I'm human, I'm not alone." He looked over at Sebastian. "There's always someone. Always a friend somewhere."

"And I'll give you another reason to do whatever it takes to stop being a bug," Sebastian said.

I looked over at him. "What?"

"No human could possibly drool as much as you

are right now," he said. He smiled like that was some great joke.

"Watch this," I said to Sebastian. I waited until I was sure I had his attention. Then I turned my back to him and spun my head around so I was staring him in the eyes. He fainted again. But he woke up on his own this time.

"What's your idea?" I asked Norman.

He clapped his hands together. "It's great. We're going to make you metamorphose. I mean, we'll make you change shape. What you said about butterflies. It made me think. Why not make a cocoon for you? It has to make you change. With luck, you'll be human when you come out."

"Or a butterfly," Sebastian said.

"No way," Norman said. But he didn't sound real sure.

I wasn't sure about that, either. But I knew I had to do something. "How can you make a cocoon?"

"Tape," Norman suggested.

"Yeah," Sebastian said. "My dad has tons of it. Let's go to my house."

"Someone will see me," I said.

"We'll carry you," Norman told me. "Sebastian has all kinds of monster models and stuff. We'll just pretend you're a dummy."

At the word *dummy*, my hand shot out. "Ouch!" Norman shouted. "Not that kind of dummy. A model. Okay?"

"Sorry." I let go of his wrist.

"Come on," Norman said to Sebastian, "you want to take the head or the legs?"

Sebastian's face went pale. He took a step away from me.

"Stop being such a baby," Norman said. "Head or legs?"

"Legs," Sebastian said, taking a deep breath. "Definitely legs."

"Grab a butterfly," Norman said. "We might need it."

Sebastian shook his head. "Not me."

Norman sighed and picked up one of his samples—a butterfly between two pieces of stiff plastic—and put it in his pocket.

I leaned back and Norman grabbed my shoulders. Sebastian picked up my legs. "Don't move," Norman said as they carried me down the stairs. "Pretend you're a dum—a model."

I held still.

"My word, what's that?" someone asked when we reached the bottom of the stairs. I figured it must be Norman's mother.

"Well, it's either Sebastian's new model or a huge

kid from my school who looks a whole lot like an insect," Norman said.

"Very funny. Just get it outside," his mother said. "It's dripping on the floor."

"Right away." I heard the door open, and then we were outside.

They ran into a couple of people along the way. I stayed still and nobody figured out I wasn't a model. We'd just reached Sebastian's house when someone shouted, "Wait! Stop!"

Twenty-one

WRAP IT UP

"Oh man. It's Bud Mellon," Sebastian said. "We're dead."

"He won't hurt you," I said. Or tried to say. My voice was more like a buzz now.

"That's my brother," Bud said, running up to us. Pit was with him.

"Ssshhhh," Norman said. "Let's talk about this inside. We're pretending he's a model."

"I got a model," Pit said, holding up his Captain Spazmodic figure.

"How'd you find us?" Norman asked.

"He ditched me yesterday to go to your house. I figured he'd done it again. I shouldn't even be coming after him, the way he ditched me. But he's my brother. And we Mellons stick together."

"Thanks," I said. It was mostly a buzz.

They carried me inside, then took me upstairs. Sebastian ran out of the room. I crawled up the wall. It felt good not having to hold still. When Sebastian came back, I crawled down and they started wrapping me in the tape. Norman explained his idea to Bud.

Bud just stood there, watching me.

"Angry?" I asked, trying very hard to say the word clearly.

Bud shook his head. "No. Just thinking."

Whoa. I'd never heard Bud say he was doing that before.

They had my legs taped by then and were starting on my body. I stood still, wondering whether this was a good idea. But I figured doing something was better than doing nothing. Hey—I thought of a joke. I was the world's biggest tapeworm.

They had my stomach done now. I crossed my hands on my chest, feeling like a mummy.

"Hold this," Norman said, putting the butterfly in my hands. "With luck, you'll mimic it and change."

Sebastian turned on his stereo. I guess, since they were wrapping me, it was wrap music. Oh man, if I became a total bug, I was really going to miss making jokes. Not that anyone ever got to hear them.

"Wait," Bud said. "It's wrong."

"What's wrong?" Norman asked.

"He copies stuff," Bud said. "Right? He's a mimic bug. That's what you told him."

Norman nodded.

"So give him the right thing to copy. We don't want him to be a butterfly. We want him to be human." Bud reached out and grabbed Captain Spazmodic from Pit.

"Hey!" Pit yelled.

"Quiet," Bud said. "Lud needs this."

"That's crazy," Sebastian said.

"Bad idea," Norman said.

They all started arguing. I could tell Bud was getting ready to throw some punches.

"Wait!" I shouted. It didn't come out that way. It was just a buzz. I couldn't make words anymore, but at least I got their attention.

Everyone turned toward me. "Let him decide," Norman said.

I looked at Norman. He was so smart. He knew more than I'd ever know. I looked at Bud. He'd never had a good idea his whole life. He got me into this whole mess in the first place. And he got me into the stupid talent show. And he'd gotten me into a thousand other types of trouble.

But it made sense.

I handed back the butterfly to Norman, then held out my hand to Bud. He gave me Captain Spazmodic. I folded my arms back together and nodded.

"Go loose around the nose and mouth," Norman said as they finished wrapping me. "Bugs don't breathe like people, but Lud might still have lungs. We don't want to suffocate him."

The last thing I saw was the four of them looking at me with worried eyes. My big brother, my little brother, and two kids I never thought I'd have anything to do with. Two kids who were helping me even though I'd never done a thing for them.

I closed my eyes. Right then, I heard Norman laughing. Man—was it all some kind of trick or joke? That was it. He was getting even with me. Getting even for the seventeen times I'd beaten him up.

His laugh rang in my ears. He'd outsmarted me.

Twenty-two

SHELLING OUT

"A bug in the program," Norman said. "I just got it. That's a good joke."

I felt someone pat my shoulder through the tape.

"He makes lots of good jokes," Bud said.

"I just never expected it," Norman said. "I guess that's why I didn't catch it right away."

They kept talking, but their voices seemed to go farther and farther away as I settled into the darkness around me.

I drifted.

It was deeper than sleep. I don't know how long it lasted. I seemed to take forever to come out of it.

"Hey. He's moving."

The voice. It was Bud. I remembered the cocoon. I pushed out against the tape.

Once I pushed my hand through the tape, it ripped easily. I stood up, feeling a bit dizzy. I couldn't see clearly. Everything was real blurry.

"Oh no," Norman said. His voice sounded very far away.

"It didn't work," Sebastian said. "I knew he shouldn't have taken the model. Now what are we going to do?"

"He's the same," Bud said. "He didn't change at all. My brother's a bug."

I didn't feel the same. I felt hot. Real hot. I couldn't seem to get any air. Everything was stuffy. Sweat rolled down my cheek.

Sweat?

I didn't think bugs sweated. Something had changed.

I tried to take a step. I heard a sharp cracking sound.

"Look," Norman cried, "it's cracking open!"

Suddenly, there was air. And light. The bug body was splitting into two pieces, falling off me. I held up my hands and looked at them. Normal. I touched my face. Normal. I'd changed. But I'd done it inside the bug.

I stepped away from the shell.

"An intact exoskeleton," Norman said, stooping down to look at what was left of the bug.

I went over to Bud. "Thanks. You were right."

He grinned. "I'm not so stupid after all."

"Nope," I told him. "Not at all."

Thwack!

"Hey!" I said after he smacked me in the head. "What was that for?"

"Just felt like it," Bud told me.

I turned to Norman. "Thanks for helping me."

He grinned. "I sort of enjoyed it. Can I assume I no longer need to carry two sets of lunch money?"

"Yeah. Or even one. From now on, I'm buying your lunch for you." I turned to Sebastian. "Thank you, too."

"My pleasure, big guy. I love monsters."

I looked at the bug skin, then reached down and grabbed Captain Spazmodic from where he was clutched in the right claw. "Here," I said, handing the figure back to Pit. "It wouldn't have happened without you."

"Smart move," Norman said. He patted Pit on the back. "You were right, Bud. I was wrong."

Thwack!

Norman smacked me on the back of the head. "Just wanted to see what it was like," he said.

"Any time," I told him. "Well, I guess we should head out." I felt funny standing in Sebastian's room, especially since until just a few hours ago, I'd hated him.

"Hey, you can hang out if you want."

I looked at Bud. He shrugged.

"Sure," I said. "We can hang out for a while."

So we stayed and looked at comic books and stuff.

A bit later, Sebastian's little brother, Rory, came in and he and Pit actually seemed to get along. As we were leaving, Norman pointed to the bug shell. "What about this?"

"You can have it," I told him. "But I need to borrow it next week."

I had plans for it.

Twenty-three

ONSTAGE

I watched the audience from behind the curtain. When they called my name and announced my act, the whole place got quiet. This was the moment I'd been afraid of. Walking out. Facing them. But I had done something to give me courage.

I stepped out. A couple kids screamed. I heard someone whisper, "Awesome costume."

Someone else said, "That can't be Lud."

I reached out and grabbed the microphone with one claw. It wasn't easy. The bug skeleton—Norman explained to me that it was really a skeleton, only on the outside—was stiff, but it fit me perfectly. Bud had drilled a couple air holes in the head, so I could breathe, and he'd made some slits so I could see through the eyes.

"Good evening," I said. "I don't know about you. But school really bugs me."

I paused and waited a second.

"As soon as the bell rings, I fly out the door."

Still dead silence. It was getting hot inside the skeleton. I thought about walking off the stage. This had been a stupid idea. Nobody was getting my jokes. I gave it one more try.

"Everyone knows I'm not a bookworm."

Someone laughed. It was Sebastian. I flinched, thinking he was laughing at me. But he slapped his knee and said, "Bookworm! That was good."

Someone else laughed. Norman.

Then a third laugh. Higher. It was Dawn. I knew she'd never laugh at me. She must have liked the joke. I could see her in the third row. She smiled. That was the other reason I'd worn the bug skeleton—to let her know it was just a costume. I didn't want her going through life thinking there were giant bugs out there.

I heard Bud laughing, too.

"At least I don't have to study for my tests," I said. "You know why?"

"Why?" a couple kids called out from the audience.

"Because I can always wing it."

A few more kids laughed.

I kept going. Soon, they were all laughing. Not at me. At my jokes. When I was done, they clapped and

cheered. I pulled open the bug shell and stepped out, taking a bow. As they clapped, I looked down at the insect I had been. I didn't think I'd need it again. Next time—and I knew there'd be a next time—I'd just go up as myself. Lud. Lud the Comedian. I'm a funny guy. That's a fact.

About the Author

David Lubar grew up in Morristown, New Jersey. His books include *Hidden Talents*, an ALA Best Book for Young Adults; *True Talents*; *Flip*, a VOYA Best Science Fiction, Fantasy, and Horror selection; the Weenies short-story collections; and the Nathan Abercrombie, Accidental Zombie series. He lives in Nazareth, Pennsylvania. You can visit him on the Web at www.david lubar.com.